The Pride Street Crew

*12*

# Make A Splash!

## Mike Wilson

*Published in association with*
The Basic Skills Agency

Hodder & Stoughton

A MEMBER OF THE H

**Acknowledgements**
*Cover: Jim Eldridge*
*Illustrations: Jim Eldridge*

Orders; please contact Bookpoint Ltd, 39 Milton Park, Abingdon, Oxon OX14 4TD. Telephone: (44) 01235 400414, Fax: (44) 01235 400454. Lines are open from 9.00–6.00, Monday to Saturday, with a 24 hour message answering service. Email address: orders@bookpoint.co.uk

*British Library Cataloguing in Publication Data*
A catalogue record for this title is available from the British Library

ISBN 0 340 77633 1

First published 2000
Impression number 10 9 8 7 6 5 4 3 2 1
Year                        2005 2004 2003 2002 2001 2000

Typeset by GreenGate Publishing Services, Tonbridge, Kent.
Printed in Great Britain for Hodder and Stoughton Educational, a division of Hodder Headline Plc, 338 Euston Road, London NW1 3BH, by Atheneum Press, Gateshead, Tyne & Wear

JOHN / BONE

WESLEY / TALL

LUKE / SKY

SIMON / CUSTARD

CARL / SPOT

'Tall, I know it will work.
It will be so cool.
Trust me.'

Tall and me are in the petrol station.
Putting air in our bike tyres.
Any second now,
the man will come out
and make us go away.

I'm looking at all the cars
in the petrol station.
Look how dirty they are!

I'm telling Tall
how we can make a bit of money.

'It's easy,' I'm saying.
'Trust me.'

But Tall doesn't trust me.

'You're rubbish, man,' he says.
'You've always got a rubbish plan
and your plans never work ...'

'This one will,' I tell him.
'This one will be a smash hit!'
Then I laugh,
'This one will make a splash!'

Tall is not happy.
So I just tell him again.

'All we need,' I say,
'is a bucket, and some water
and some soap and stuff.
Then we just stand
and wait for them to come to us.'

'I'm not cleaning cars, Luke,' says Tall.
'It's just a rubbish thing to do.'

'But it's money,' I say.
'Money in your pocket.'

Tall wants a Discman
and he's got no money.
But he can get the money
if he cleans cars with me.

'Money,' I say again.
'Money for CDs,
and CD players ...
Money for Man United goal-keeper shirts ...'

I've got him.

'All right,' he says.
'We'll give it a go
on Friday, after school.'

'It won't take long, Tall,' I go on.
'I know it will work.
Trust me.'

Then he looks at me, sort of funny.

'What?' I ask.

'Trust you?' he says.
'What, like Lizzy trusted you?'

That hurt.
There was no need for that.

Me and Lizzy had a bust up.
I hadn't seen her for a while.
I wanted to, but ...
she didn't want to see me.

Wesley seemed to think it was all my fault.
But it wasn't.
It wasn't *all* my fault ...
If anyone was to blame,
it was Tamsin Taylor.

She started it.

8

Tall and me agree to meet
on Friday, after school.
We go to the traffic lights
on Pond Street.

It's the main street out of town.
There's lots of traffic
at that time of day.

I bring my Dad's car kit –
all his rags and stuff.
Tall brings a bucket of water
on his bike.
By the time he gets there,
there's not much water left in the bucket.

'Man, my feet are soaking wet!'
Tall says.

He throws down his bike.
He looks at me like it's my fault.

I take no notice.

The lights are on red,
so I go up to the first car.
I go round to the driver's side.

'Clean your windscreen, sir?'

I lean in and smile.

'Push off, or I'll call the police,'
the man says.

I go back to Tall.

He asks,
'What did he say?'

I say,
'Er … He said the car is brand new …
It's not dirty yet …'

Tall gives me his 'I don't trust you' look again.

After a bit,
the lights go red again.
A red sports car pulls up.

I say to Tall,
'Go on.
It's your turn.'

He says,
'No. It's a woman.
You go.'

So I go over to the woman
in the red sports car.

I lean in and smile.
'Clean your windscreen for you?'

'Sure, my love,' she says. 'Why not?'

I run back for the bucket
and a sponge,
and Tall.

He does one side,
I do the other.
It takes us twenty seconds
to get the windscreen looking like new.

I stand back,
and put the bucket down.

Just then,
the lights go green,
and the red sports car revs up.

The woman smiles and waves.
'Thanks, love!' she says.
In six seconds, she is half a mile away,
speeding past the next set of lights.

'*Thanks, love!*' says Tall.

'Shut it, Tall,' I say.
'Just shut it!'

'You forgot a bit,' he says.
'Quite a good bit …
You see, *we* clean the windscreens …
And *they* give us some …'

'OK!' I shout at him, 'OK!'
'Let's see *you* do one then!'

Tall steps out into the road.
He speaks to a lady
in a little old car.
Then he gets to work
on her windscreen.

When the lights go green,
the lady holds some money
out of her window.
A brand new twenty pound note.

'Have you got any change?'
she asks.

There's a look of horror on Wesley's face.
We haven't got any money at all.

The car behind pips his horn.
'Hey, kid!' a man shouts.
'Get out the way
before I run you down!'

The woman says,
'Look, I'm sorry,
but I've got to go.
I'll be here, same time next week.
You can have your 50p then.'

And then she pulls slowly away.

In the first hour,
Tall and me do eight windscreens.

We've got 73 pence,
some Spanish money,
and a coupon for a Garden Centre.

Wesley has just been home,
to get more water.
So I say I'll do the next car.

Big mistake.

I carry the bucket over to the lights.
A car pulls up, really slowly.
It's got L-plates,
and a sign: El Passo Driving School.

A man with a clip-board
is sitting next to the driver.
He's talking to her.

Oh no.
It's Lizzy.

It's the first time I've seen her in weeks.

The window is shut.
I put my face up close
and smile.

It doesn't work.
I'm trying to smile.
But I know I'm doing the face I do
when Dad makes me listen to his CDs.

'Hello, Lizzy!' I shout.
'When can I see you?'

Lizzy looks away.
She says something
to the man with the clip-board.
He says something to her.

Lizzy looks at me.
Her look says, Not now!
Go away!

Then I get an idea.
A really stupid idea.
I put my bucket down
and walk round in front of the car.

I fold my arms.
I just stand there and smile at her.
I'm not moving
until she says she'll see me.

The lights go green.
All the cars get ready to go.
I don't move.

Lizzy revs the car.
She drives forward three inches.
And stops.

I don't move.

The car behind pips his horn.
Nobody moves.

The lights go back to red.

22

The man with the clip-board says something.
Then he gets out of the car.

'Look, you little prat ...' he says to me.

But Lizzy has jumped out of the car as well.
She grabs the bucket of water.

She's got that look in her eye –
she's wild.
I remember that time she hit Carl
and left him flat on the floor.

She comes up to me and says,
'I've just failed my driving test!
Thanks to you!'

And she lets me have it.

I want to think of something cool and clever
to call after her.
But all I can think of
is freezing cold water,
going into my shirt, and my jeans.

And then my pants.

Meanwhile,
Lizzy has burst into tears.
The man takes her back to the car.
He puts her in the seat he'd been in.
Then he gets in the driver's side,
and drives them both away.

I stand there for a bit,
letting the misery
soak into my bones.

Wesley says, 'Luke …
You got my feet wet again.'

We pack up our things.
Then we split the money we made.
Wesley takes the 73 pence.
He lets me have the Spanish money.

'Luke,' he says, 'do me a favour.
Next time you have an idea,
about making some money,
about *making a splash* …
Tell me, right?
So I can stand well back …'

When I get home,
Mum says,
'What happened to you?'

I tell her the whole story.

I hold out a small piece of paper.
It's all wet and soggy.

'What's this?' she asks.

It's the coupon for the Garden Centre.

'Thanks love,' she says.
'Now go and get out of those clothes,
and let me wash them.'

I head for the stairs.

'Luke,' Mum calls after me.
'You say Lizzy was crying.
She must be really upset …

'Deep down,
she must really love you …'

# Shop Till You Drop

## John Goodwin

*Published in association with*
The Basic Skills Agency

Hodder & Stoughton

A MEMBER OF THE HODDER HEADLINE GROUP

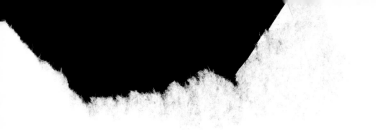

**Acknowledgements**
*Cover: Barry Downard*
*Illustrations: Ruth Thomlevold*

Orders: please contact Bookpoint Ltd, 130 Milton Park, Abingdon, Oxon OX14
4SB. Telephone: (44) 01235 827720, Fax: (44) 01235 400454. Lines are open from
9.00–6.00, Monday to Saturday, with a 24 hour message answering service. You
can also order through our website: www.hodderheadline.co.uk.

*British Library Cataloguing in Publication Data*
A catalogue record for this title is available from The British Library

ISBN 0 340 87661 1

First published 2003
Impression number  10 9 8 7 6 5 4 3 2 1
Year                         2007 2006 2005 2004 2003

Typeset by SX Composing DTP, Rayleigh, Essex.
Printed in Great Britain for Hodder & Stoughton Educational, a division of
Hodder Headline, 338 Euston Road, London NW1 3BH by Athenaeum Press,
Gateshead, Tyne and Wear.